THE YELLOW HOUSE MYSTERY

The Alden children discover a mystery at the run-down yellow house on Surprise Island. Years ago a man vanished from the house. Nobody knew how or why. Now the children are determined to learn the real story. A trail of clues leads them on a new adventure, and an old mystery is solved!

THE BOXCAR CHILDREN
GRAPHIC NOVELS

THE BOXCAR CHILDREN
SURPRISE ISLAND
THE YELLOW HOUSE MYSTERY
MYSTERY RANCH
MIKE'S MYSTERY
BLUE BAY MYSTERY

Gertrude Chandler Warner's

THE BOXCAR CHILDREN

THE YELLOW HOUSE MYSTERY

Adapted by Rob M. Worley
Illustrated by Mike Dubisch

Henry Alden

Jessie Alden

Watch

Violet Alden

Benny Alden

Visit us at www.albertwhitman.com.

Adapted by Rob M. Worley
Illustrated by Mike Dubisch
Colored by Wes Hartman
Lettered by Johnny Lowe
Edited by Stephanie Hedlund
Interior layout and design by Kristen Fitzner Denton
Cover art by Mike Dubisch
Book design and packaging by Shannon Eric Denton

Library of Congress Cataloging-in-Publication Data

Worley, Rob M.
The yellow house mystery / adapted by Rob M. Worley ; illustrated by Mike Dubisch.
p. cm. -- (Gertrude Chandler Warner's boxcar children)
ISBN 978-1-60270-588-3
[1. Orphans--Fiction. 2. Family--Fiction. 3. Mystery and detective stories.] I. Dubisch, Michael, ill. II. Warner, Gertrude Chandler, 1890-1979. Yellow house mystery. III. Title.
PZ7.W887625Yel 2009
[E]--dc22

2008036114

Gertrude Chandler Warner's
THE
BOXCAR
CHILDREN
GRAPHIC
NOVELS

THE YELLOW HOUSE MYSTERY

Contents

THE CAVE
Just six months ago, the Alden children had spent their summer on Surprise Island. There they met their cousin Joe, an archaeologist, and discovered a cave full of important artifacts.
Now it was spring, and Benny had just finished a mysterious phone call.
Henry! Violet! Jess! Come quick!
Joe just telephoned! The men are going to blast the cave on Surprise Island. We have to hurry and go over.
Mr. Alden and Captain Daniel took the children to Surprise Island immediately.
There's Joe now. Who is that girl that's with him?
That's not a girl. That's a lady!
Hello! This is Alice Wells. She's here to help with the dig.
Let's go right off and see them blast!

This is going to be fun for you, Benny. The men are going to let you push the handle to set off the blast.
Oh boy!
And with that Benny cleared the top off the cave.
KA-BOOOOOM!
What a noise that was!
The big rocks became small rocks. The workers began clearing them right away. Joe explained that it would take days to remove all the rocks, so the children returned home.
I think Joe likes Alice. I think he's going to marry her.
What? How can you tell? Joe just met her today!
Oh, no. Joe and Alice went to school together when they were children. She's just returned to help Joe at the cave.
I wish Joe would get married. He must be awfully lonesome living by himself.
I think Benny is right. But let's not say anything to them. Let's wait and see what happens.

A WEDDING
All spring, the children went to the island to help. One day, Joe, Henry, and Benny stopped to rest at a yellow house.
Let's go into this house sometime.
Your grandfather never likes to talk about this house. I think it has a mystery.
Joe, let's tell them our news!
Maybe we can guess!
You and Joe are getting married! Aren't you?
It's true! Look at your ring!
When school let out for the summer, Joe and Alice got married. What a wedding it was! Alice was very lovely in her beautiful white dress. Violet played her violin.
After the wedding, Joe and Alice left for their honeymoon.
I do hope Alice and Joe will still spend time with us.
Mrs. McGregor is sad even when she smiles.

With Joe away, the children started to think of summer plans. Henry decided to ask Grandfather about the yellow house on Surprise Island.

I suppose you ought to know about the yellow house. My father used to keep race horses on the island. A man named Bill took care of them.

Bill was a good man, but he was weak...

"Bill lived on the island with his wife, Margaret. One night Margaret heard a strange noise. Bill told her it was the waves.

"One night, Bill went out to the barn and never came back.

"Margaret saw that the horses had been fed. But Bill and his rowboat were gone.

"They found Bill's rowboat a few days later. It was tied up at another dock about a mile away on the mainland.

"Margaret told the police about the noises and paint smell. They went all over the little yellow house searching for clues.
"We put notices in the newspaper for two years. Nothing ever came of it."
I'm so sorry for Margaret. She must be old now.
She seems very old to you, I know. She is Mrs. McGregor.
Mrs. McGregor!
Grandfather, couldn't we go into the little yellow house? We might find something.
You may go. But don't talk about this to Mrs. McGregor yet.
Soon Joe and Alice returned home. Before they'd even gotten into the house the children were telling them about the mystery of the little yellow house.
I've wondered about that house myself. I'd like to go inside.
We've waited for you to go with us.
Captain Daniel brought the whole family to Surprise Island. Mr. Alden unlocked the yellow house for the first time in years.

Let's look around and see what could make a strange noise.
I'm going to check every brick on this chimney.
A paintbrush! Remember the paint smell? I think this was used on the fireplace.
A pen. Some old writing paper.
That's all.
Joe gave Benny one of his digging tools. Benny carefully tapped each brick in the fire-place with his little hammer, listening for anything strange.
TOK! TOK!
Joe! This one sounds different!
Yes, this brick has certainly been taken out.

What did I tell you? Look! There's a letter in the hole!
"Dear Bill, Thanks for the money. I can make it three times as much if you will help me. Some friends of mine know how. Meet me at your little house in Maine. (Bear Trail) Then you can pay Mr. A. and get your part of the rest sure. Look in the tin box. Hide this. S.M."
Now we have a real mystery.
I remember one other thing. Just before Bill disappeared, he sold two fine race horses. But he never gave my father the money.
I always thought his brother, Sam, got it.
But the week after Bill disappeared, Sam was killed by a car.
I know Bear Trail. I went there when I was fifteen years old.
So you did!

Yes, yes! I know what you want. You want to go up to Maine and hunt for Bill.
You always let us do things in the summer when there isn't any school. Joe and Alice want to go, too!
There was a lot of noise in the Alden house after that. Soon they were loading food and gear in the station wagon for the trip.
What a family! Always doing something exciting!
After driving several hours, they arrived at a store. The owner, Mr. Long, helped them get everything they'd need.
I can fix you up! You'll need two canoes and some tents too.
LON
LIVE BAIT
Thank you, Mr. Long. Say, we're looking for an old man who is lost. Bill McGregor.
Never heard of him. I'm sorry.
When everything was loaded, Mr. Long gave the canoes a last push into the lake. The canoes began to slide through the smooth blue water.

COMPANY IN THE WOODS
Look, Joe! There's a tree in the water.
That's no tree, Benny! That's a moose swimming across the lake.
Henry! Look! A moose!
They paddled very fast all day. Just as Henry was starting to feel tired...
We'll make camp up there.
And don't forget we've got company coming.
We'll have a lot of work to do once we get there.
Take everything out of the canoes and put it in this open place. Here's one of the best camping places in Maine!
Hello, Mr. Hill. Mr. Long tells me you're one of the best guides in Maine.
I suppose you are Joe Alden. Want me to build your tent and cook you some corn bread?

Mr. Hill told the children to find branches of a certain shape. When Henry and Benny brought them, he fashioned them into a camping stove.
Now we can boil water here for cleaning or cooking. And we can hang more than one pot.
Mr. Hill began to make a shelter-half to keep the wind from the fire.
This would keep the rain out, too, if we had any rain.
Mr. Hill then cooked a meal of corn bread, ham, and eggs for the hungry travelers.
How delicious the ham and eggs are. And the corn bread too.
I'm so sleepy I could go to sleep standing up!

The children stayed very quiet. The bear did not seem to notice them. It was only interested in the ham that it found in the trees.

Just then Mr. Hill flashed a light in the bear's face. The bear ran off into the woods. The children did not know that Mr. Hill and the bear were good friends. The bear knew that he would find food wherever Mr. Hill was.

In the morning everyone packed up camp. Mr. Hill made breakfast and then said good-bye.

There's a lumber camp up the river. That's our next stop.

THE LUMBER CAMP
Later, Joe revealed that Mr. Hill had brought them fishing rods!
We fish with Grey Ghosts that look like flies.
Can I try?
Benny tried his hand at casting.
Alice!
I'm sorry, Alice! I don't see how I did that.
WHAP!
I should have been watching. Everyone does that their first time.
Benny tried again and again. Eventually he got the hang of it. Soon they had enough fish and it was time to paddle on.
That afternoon, they could hear the lumber camp. They could hear axes and a great crash of a tree falling down.
The men at the camp roll the logs into the water and they float down by themselves.

Soon the boss at the logging camp waved them ashore.
Welcome! Would you like to share dinner with us lumber men?
Stay as long as you want. You like beans?
We love beans but we got a lot of fish. I caught this one, and this one...
When dinner was ready, Cookie let Benny ring the bell. The lumber men came crashing through the bushes.
They ate dinner of fish, beans, and quick bread. They met a lumber man named Bill, but he was too young to be the Bill they were looking for.
That night, Henry heard many loud squeals and what sounded like men sawing trees.
It's porcupines!
What a noise! They sound like pigs and men sawing wood.
In the morning, the family had breakfast with the lumber men. The boss agreed to ask around about Bill McGregor. Then, the Aldens set off for the Old Village.

ALMOST STARVING
Soon they had come to the end of the lake and had to carry the canoes to another lake. It wasn't very far but they had a lot to carry.
Carrying isn't as much fun as I thought it would be!
They paddled a long way on this new lake. Very suddenly the sky went dark gray and the wind began to blow. Out of nowhere, a rainstorm came.
Get to shore, Henry! Just as fast as you can! Land between those two large trees!
Pull our canoe out of Joe's way, so he can land, too!
As Joe paddled in, a big wave hit his canoe sideways. It washed the bags of food and dishes into the lake.
All our food is gone.
Are we going to starve, Joe?
Starve? No, but I guess we are going to be very hungry.
Just **almost** starve.

While Joe worked to start a fire, Benny and Alice discovered one bag of food that hadn't drifted away.
Are you warm enough, Violet?
I'm all right.
I can get it. I'm as wet as I can be already.
Oh, **Benny!** How glad everyone will be!
When they got back the fire was started. Joe took the potatoes from the bag and put them on the fire.
They will burn, but never mind. We have to eat something.
It was a tough night, but the Aldens were happy to have survived the storm.
We may not find old Bill. No one seems to have heard of him. I just don't want you to be disappointed.
It's alright, Joe. I had fun just camping!
Oh, yes. We've all had fun!

They paddled hard all morning. Benny fished to pass the time and caught a big lake trout. By noon they arrived at Old Village.
Right away, Joe asked if there was any place the group could get a meal.
You can eat at Jim's Place in town. I run it myself. I'm Jim Carr. I'll cook you hamburger if you--
Oh, **hamburger!** I want hamburger!
Oh, I do feel better! I'm ready for anything!
I think Violet ought to sleep in a real bed tonight.
There's a little old house I take care of across the street, if you want to stay for the night.
Then it's settled. We'll stay the night.
I'll get that house ready. There are lots of interesting things to see in Old Village. There's an old hermit over in the woods. Lives all alone. And the Indians up the road make baskets to sell.
Maybe they've heard of Bill.

A HUNT FOR BENNY
My, doesn't she work fast! See her fingers fly.
I wish I could learn to do that.
I'll teach you. My name is Rita.
Wonderful, Violet!
Benny? Oh, **where** is Benny?
BENNY!
Oh, what has happened to Benny?
The village is small and I'm a good tracker. We'll find him.
BENNY!
He went this way. I can see where he stepped. This is the way to the old hermit's cabin. Now call him.
Ben-NY!

This is the hermit's cabin. If we scare him, he'll run away, and then he won't help us.
Thank you for telling me your name.
Your family must be worried. Come on, I'll take you back.
Oh, **Benny!**
The hermit is nice. His name is Dave Hunter.
I think Dave Hunter wants us to go. That's just how he is.
You can stay in this house as long as you want. Walk right in.
It's small, but most campers don't mind sleeping two or three to a room.
Thank you, Jim.

THE BOX AGAIN
The Aldens spread the bedrolls onto cots in the house. They cooked Benny's trout and had a good meal. Still, they weren't ready for bed.
You know, I feel as if something will happen soon.
I feel that way too.
That's funny. I do too. It's as if we had a clue and didn't know it.
The next morning, the family had breakfast and then went to thank Rita again.
Don't run away again, little boy. You make too much trouble for the hermit.
For the **hermit?**
Dave Hunter was upset. My father says he was a very nice young man once. He built that house you're staying in.
One night, he fought with some mean men. Then, he went into the woods and has stayed there ever since.
Jessie, maybe Dave Hunter is Bill.
The children returned to the old house and told everyone what Rita had said.
Pretend you're in the yellow house on Surprise Island!
There's the same fireplace. That window is in the same place.

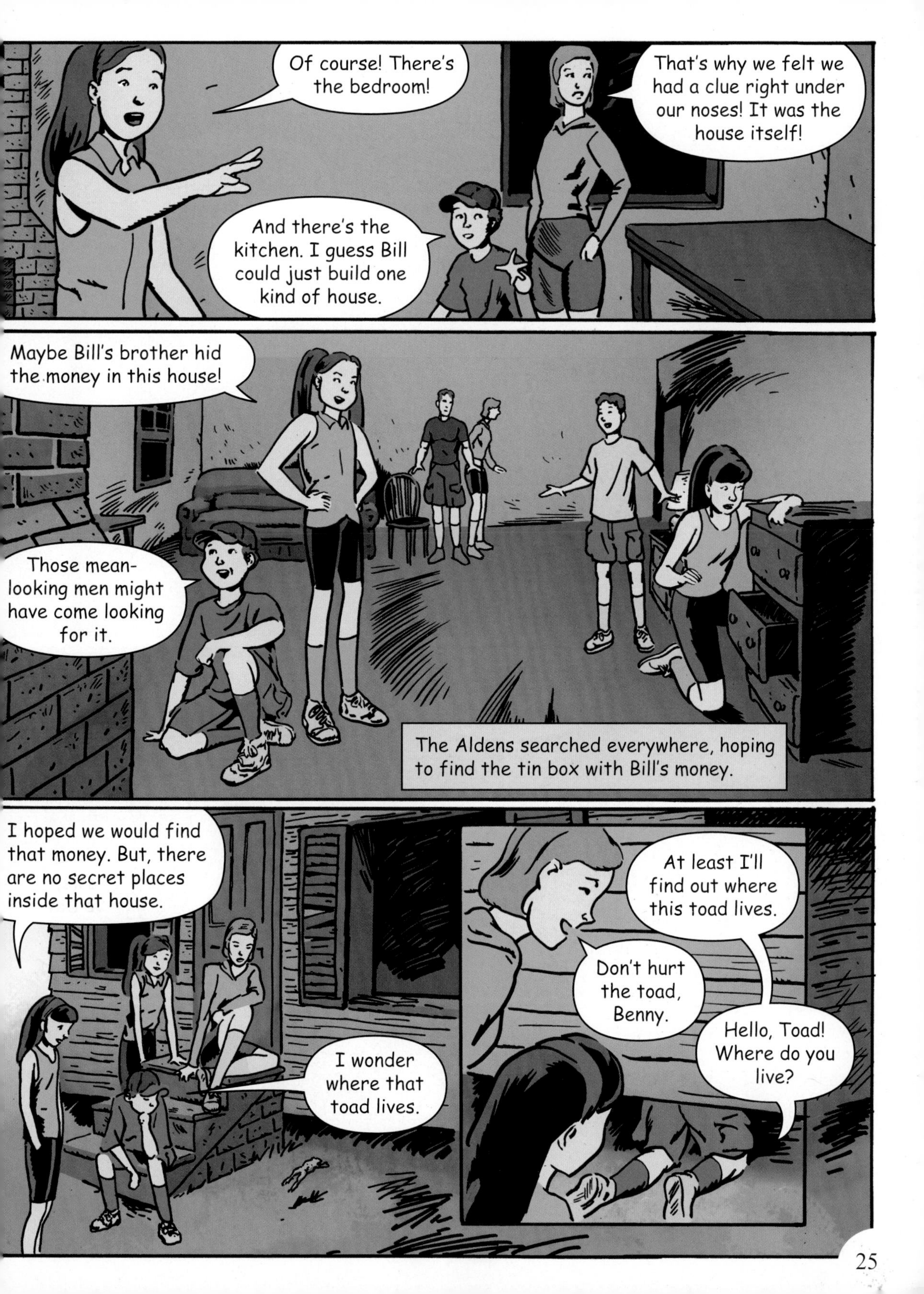
Of course! There's the bedroom!
That's why we felt we had a clue right under our noses! It was the house itself!
And there's the kitchen. I guess Bill could just build one kind of house.
Maybe Bill's brother hid the money in this house!
Those mean-looking men might have come looking for it.
The Aldens searched everywhere, hoping to find the tin box with Bill's money.
I hoped we would find that money. But, there are no secret places inside that house.
I wonder where that toad lives.
At least I'll find out where this toad lives.
Don't hurt the toad, Benny.
Hello, Toad! Where do you live?

Henry! There's a tin box here! I found it!
They counted the money and found four thousand dollars. Joe thought it was time to talk to the hermit again.
The hermit is Dave Hunter. And Dave Hunter is Bill.
I think so, too.
When the hermit saw the visitors, he ran into his cabin.
Bill!

Bill, Grandfather wants you to come home, and so does Mrs. McGregor.
He means Margaret.
Margaret is dead.
They said there was a fire and the barn burned and Margaret died trying to save the horses.
No, Margaret is alive.
Bill explained that he had no reason to go back to Surprise Island when he thought Margaret had died. When Joe told him the truth, he could hardly believe his ears.
Bill felt better after eating.
I suppose Mrs. McGregor won't know you with that beard.
Benny!
My beard can be cut off. Then I will look like Bill McGregor. I think I would like to go home with you.

STARTING FOR HOME
The next morning, Mr. Long and his son arrived.
It's the station wagon!
Ha ha! You didn't hear me make this plan with Mr. Long, did you? I made a lot of plans up at the store that first day.
The little house was soon full of people rushing around, rolling up bedrolls. They packed a big lunch. There was one more thing to take care of before they left...
Now I will look like Bill McGregor for the first time in a long time.
Mrs. McGregor will like you better this way.
Mr. Long and his son began the canoe trip back to the store. The Aldens went home in the car.
On the long drive, Bill told them his story.
"I sold two fine race horses for your great grandfather. My brother Sam told me to give him the money, and he could make three times as much.
"Sam hid the money, but then he was killed. I hunted for his tin box, but I could never find it. His friends didn't know where it was, either.
"I couldn't go home, so I went to live in the woods."

After a long day of driving, the family arrived home.
It's my Margaret! She has the same beautiful blue eyes!
Bill!
It's all right, Bill! It's all right!
Mrs. McGregor wasn't the only one happy to see them!

A HAPPY HOME
Bill, how was your brother going to make the money three times as much?
I didn't know myself at first. Later I found out he was going to give it to his friends to bet on the horse races.
Oh, but he might have lost it all!
"His friends were bad people, I'm afraid.
"They didn't want me to return home, so they told me Margaret had died.
"After Sam was killed, they came to my house in Maine. They hunted for the tin box.
"That's when I went to live alone forever."
You can live right here, now, Bill.
I can help with the horses. Do you still keep horses?
Yes, we have two, but you will rest a long time before doing any work.

Violet had an idea. Mr. Alden could use the money from the tin box to fix up the yellow house on Surprise Island.
Mr. and Mrs. McGregor could live there in the summer and the children could visit whenever they wanted.
That's what they did. Soon, the yellow house was a happy place again.

ABOUT THE CREATOR

Gertrude Chandler Warner was born on April 16, 1890, in Putnam, Connecticut. In 1918, Warner began teaching at Israel Putnam School. As a teacher, she discovered that many readers who liked an exciting story could not find books that were both easy and fun to read. She decided to try to meet this need. In 1942, *The Boxcar Children* was published for these readers.

Warner drew on her own experience to write *The Boxcar Children*. As a child she spent hours watching trains go by on the tracks near her family home. She often dreamed about what it would be like to live in a caboose or freight car—just as the Alden children do.

When readers asked for more Alden adventures, Warner began additional stories. While the mystery element is central to each of the books, she never thought of them as strictly juvenile mysteries. She liked to stress the Aldens' independence. Henry, Jessie, Violet, and Benny go about most of their adventures with as little adult supervision as possible—something that delights young readers.

During her lifetime, Warner received hundreds of letters from fans as she continued the Aldens' adventures, writing nineteen Boxcar Children books in all. After her death in 1979, her publisher, Albert Whitman and Company, carried on Warner's vision. Today, the Boxcar Children series has more than 100 books.